Monkey's Magic Pipe

Written by Pat Thomson

Illustrated by Alessandra Cimatoribus

OXFORD
UNIVERSITY PRESS

Long ago, in a faraway forest, lived a monster.
He lived in a cave of bones.

He was huge.

He was hairy.

He was hungry.

One morning, the Monster went into the forest with his hunting bag.

He sang in his horrible voice,

"I'm going to eat you. Wait and see.
I'm the Monster. Beware of me!"

Snake slid away.
Parrot flew off.
Panther hid.

The Monster went to the
drinking pool.

He sat and waited.

He had hairy arms for catching.

He had big, yellow teeth for crunching.

"I am the best at waiting," he said.

As he sat in a bush by the pool,
he sang in his horrible voice,
"*I'm going to eat you. Wait and see.*
I'm the Monster. Beware of me!"

Snake was first to come to drink.

As she slid into the pool, the Monster pounced.

"Got you!" shouted the Monster. "Into my bag."

Snake was trapped.

Parrot was next to come to the pool.

As he flew down, the Monster grabbed him.

"Got you!" shouted the Monster. "Into my bag."

Parrot was trapped.

Then Panther slipped out of the shadows.

He was strong, but the Monster was stronger.

"Got you!" shouted the Monster. "Into my bag."

Even Panther was trapped.

"I shall eat them all," roared the Monster,
as he set off back to his cave of bones.
The bag bumped along behind him.
"I am the best at hunting!" he said.

The Monster saw Monkey
sitting under a tree.
"Yum," he said. "Pudding!"
Monkey had a pipe in her
little paw. She looked at the
hunting bag.

Monkey knew her friends were inside, but she was clever and had an idea to set them free.

"Monster," she called, "you are the best dancer in the forest. This new tune is just for you."

"I must be the best dancer,"
said the Monster, "because I am
the best at everything."
He pointed his hairy toe.
"Play for me," he said.

13

Monkey played and the Monster danced.
Then Monkey stopped.

"It's no good," she said sadly.
"What a pity. You dance so well."

"What do you mean?" roared the Monster.
"You need a partner," said Monkey.

"I have one," said the Monster, and dragged
Snake out of his bag.

The Monster put Snake around his neck and
danced and danced.

"Good," said Monkey. "Now change partners."

The Monster opened his bag again
and took out Parrot.
Snake slid away.

Parrot just flapped and screeched. He was not a good dancer.

The Monster had to dance around him.

"I am the best at dancing," the Monster said.

"Change partners," called Monkey.
The Monster opened his bag again.
He pulled Panther out by his tail.

Parrot flew off.

18

Panther struggled and snapped.
The Monster danced faster and faster.
He stamped his hairy feet and clicked
his claws.

"Change partners," called Monkey.

Panther sprang into the bushes.
The Monster looked in his hunting bag.

"My bag is empty," he roared.
The leaves shook on every tree.

The Monster chased Monkey,
puffing and panting.

But he was so tired he could hardly
sing his song…

"I'm going to eat you. Wait and see.
I'm the Monster. Beware of me!"

"Not today," said Monkey.
"Today, Monkey is the best of all!"

Monkey skipped away, playing her pipe.
And all the animals who heard it danced.

And what happened to the Monster?

He was so tired, he lay down in his cave of bones and snored until the bones rattled.

If you ever find his cave…

Don't go in!

Once upon a time...

The end.